SUPER FLY

SUPER FLY

The World's Smallest Superhero!

Todd H. Doodler

BLOOMSBURY
NEW YORK   LONDON   NEW DELHI   SYDNEY

First published in the United States of America in May 2015
by Bloomsbury Children's Books
www.bloomsbury.com

Bloomsbury is a registered trademark of Bloomsbury Publishing Plc

For information about permission to reproduce selections from this book, write to
Permissions, Bloomsbury Children's Books, 1385 Broadway, New York, New York 10018
Bloomsbury books may be purchased for business or promotional use. For information on bulk
purchases please contact Macmillan Corporate and Premium Sales Department at
specialmarkets@macmillan.com

Library of Congress Cataloging-in-Publication Data
Doodler, Todd H.
Super Fly : the world's smallest superhero! / by Todd H. Doodler.
pages   cm
Summary: When fourth-grader Eugene, a small and nerdy mild-mannered housefly, becomes
the world's smallest superhero, he takes on Crazy Cockroach and his army of insect baddies.
ISBN 978-1-61963-378-0 (paperback) • ISBN 978-1-61963-379-7 (hardcover)
ISBN 978-1-61963-380-3 (e-book)
[1. Superheroes—Fiction. 2. Flies—Fiction. 3. Insects—Fiction. 4. Bullying—Fiction.] I. Title.
PZ7.D7247Su 2015   [Fic]—dc23   2014029077

Book design by Nicole Gastonguay
Printed and bound in the U.S.A. by Thomson-Shore Inc., Dexter, Michigan
2 4 6 8 10 9 7 5 3 1 (paperback)
2 4 6 8 10 9 7 5 3   (hardcover)

To my little larva, Elle, who for some reason thinks I'm her superhero!

CONTENTS

SUPER FLY

1

Meet the Flysteins

Eugene Flystein lived at 851 Rumbling Rock Road with his parents, Dean and Maureen, and his little sister, Elle. The Flysteins had just moved into the neighborhood a few days before the new school year. Eugene was

STINKOPOLIS

going to be in fourth grade; Elle would be in second.

Eugene was having a hard time with the move because he loved his old neighborhood. But he knew the move was necessary. Mr. Flystein had gotten a new job in the busy, bug-centric city of Stinkopolis, an insect community on the eastern edge of the city dump.

Eugene's dad was a scientist, who earned his reputation by creating inventions. He was most famous for the "Poop-A-Rama," which

made everyday objects smell like, well, you know. It was the perfect appliance for any housefly household.

Eugene's mom doted on her little Flysteins, making sure they kept their bedrooms extra filthy and that they ate a well-balanced diet of garbage and anything that stunk. Delicious!

Eugene Flystein (if the name doesn't rhyme, you're saying it wrong) wasn't like most flies his age.

Flies typically hate books, but even at an early age Eugene Flystein loved to read. While the other neighborhood maggots were outside playing ball, Eugene was inside reading. *Lord of the Flies* was his favorite book.

Eugene's other idea of fun was helping his dad work on new inventions. Eugene's brain could solve any problem. Well, with the exception of flying. He was a terrible flyer. Have you ever heard of a fly that couldn't fly? Of course not, it's crazy! Other bugs picked on him because of it. No one really understood him, except Elle.

The thing about Elle was that she paid attention to the little things. She noticed when Eugene helped her with home-

work. She noticed when Eugene was nice to baby bugs in the dirt box. And she noticed when Eugene would help elderly bugs cross the street.

Elle also noticed that, for as smart as Eugene was, he hated being the new bug in school. He knew he just had to get through the first day, which is always the toughest. He and Elle were going to be attending Brown Barge Elementary, which was a brown pile of yuck floating in a broken toilet in the center of town. But that wasn't happening until the next morning.

Tonight the Flysteins were going to the circus. And not just any circus . . . the **FLEA CIRCUS!**

2

The Flea Circus

Eugene's parents had decided everyone needed a night out before the first day of school to calm their nerves, so they all went to see *The Greatest Bug Show on Earth: The Fantastic Flea Circus!*

Elle sat right next to Eugene so they could share a piece of stale popcorn with spoiled butter on top.

There were acrobat fleas swinging from the trapeze, daredevil fleas being shot out of cannons, and balancing fleas walking tight-ropes. There were trick fleas juggling and doing somersaults, clown fleas riding uni-cycles, and bouncing fleas doing tricks on trampolines. It was *flea*-tastic!

High-flying, death-defying, wondrous displays of acrobatics impressed Eugene and Elle. Their favorite performer was a little acrobat and trapeze artist that looked to be about the same age as Eugene.

"He's just a kid!" shouted Eugene. "Can you imagine being that good at something at our age?"

"Yes, I can," said Elle. "Because you're already good at everything!"

Eugene smiled. Elle always said nice things like that, but he couldn't see why she thought he was so great.

That night, just before Elle fell asleep, Eugene stuck his head in the door and said, "Good luck tomorrow, little sister."

"Thanks," said Elle. "And good luck to you tomorrow, big brother."

That night they both dreamed they were part of the wonderful flea circus.

Which is impossible because flies can't be fleas, and there is no such thing as a fly circus.

But even flies can dream.

3

Nice Flies Finish Last

Eugene's first day of school began on the bus, which smelled like stale corn chips and stinky armpits. Elle sat up front with some younger bugs while Eugene grabbed an empty seat near the back of the bus where the fourth and fifth graders sat. He'd just started designing a new robot, one that could do homework, when his morning took a turn for the worse.

"Hey, McFly! You're in my seat!" boomed a voice from behind Eugene. Eugene turned to see the biggest, loudest, scariest cockroach

he'd ever seen. There was no way this was a
kid cockroach. He looked like a wrestler or a
pro football player. He was huge!

"Oh, I'm sorry," said Eugene. "I sat here
because no one was here."

"That's because I was busy throwing Sid
Spider out the emergency doors at the back

of the bus," said the giant roach while crack-
ing his forelegs.

After a moment of awkward silence,
Eugene moved to a new seat, cramming in
with some fruit flies.

"Oh my god, I love your outfit!" said a
fashionably dressed fruit fly named Francine.
"Don't let that mean cockroach bother you.
Cornelius C. Roach is the biggest bully in
school. He doesn't like anybody."

"Hey, McFly!" Cornelius said, coming after
Eugene again. "I wasn't done talking to you."

Before Eugene could blink, Cornelius had lifted him out of his seat by his wings and dangled the fly upside down out the window.

"Get ready for your head to be dunked in toilet water!" said the big bully bug.

"Put my brother down!" came a small voice. Eugene recognized it immediately as Elle's.

"Who's this pipsqueak?" asked Cornelius.

"Put him down or face my wrath!" declared Elle, and the whole bus howled with laughter.

Fortunately for Eugene and Elle, the bus stopped abruptly. They had arrived at school. Cornelius pulled the terrified fly back into the bus.

"You got lucky this time, McFart!" said Cornelius. "I'll be watching you and your little brat sister." Cornelius stormed off the bus, pushing bugs down and shoving them aside as he went.

Eugene and Elle were the last two off the bus.

"Are you okay?" asked Elle.

"I'm fine, thanks," said Eugene. "Let's hurry or we'll be late." He helped Elle find her class before looking for his own.

Eugene beat the tardy bell to Mrs. Tiger Moth's fourth-grade classroom, only to discover he was going to be stuck with Cornelius all year, who was sitting near the back of the room.

"Are you kidding me?" Eugene said under his breath. "That giant cockroach is only in fourth grade? What are they feeding him?" Eugene took a seat by the door, just in case he needed to make a quick getaway.

Mrs. Tiger Moth began calling roll.

"Precious Butterfly."

"Here," said Precious.

"Bubba Beetle."

"Here," said Bubba.

"Carlos Caterpillar."

"Present," said Carlos.

"Reed Centipede."

"Yo," said Reed.

"Cornelius C. Roach."

"Cornelius C. Roach."

"Cornelius C. Roach."

Cornelius didn't answer because he was too busy giving Eugene the stink-eye. Eugene pretended not to notice.

Later that same day in gym class, Coach Caterpillar decided to start the year with a weight-lifting competition to test everyone's strength. Eugene knew he wouldn't be the strongest bug in class, but he hoped to be somewhere in the middle where he could blend in and go unnoticed.

Cornelius went first and everyone cheered him on, mostly because they were afraid of what he'd do to them if they didn't. Of course the King Kong of roaches came in first place. He barely beat Andy Ant, but that's because ants are really strong for their size.

Eugene came in last. Dead last. He couldn't even lift the bar. This day was turning up roses for Eugene—meaning it was horrible, because flies hate the smell of flowers.

"Great job, Cornelius!" said Eugene, hoping that if he was nice, Cornelius might cut him some slack.

"Shut up, nerd, before I crack you like a walnut!" said Cornelius.

Eugene thought it was a reasonable request if it kept him from being pummeled. As they lined up to go back to class, Cornelius snatched Eugene's "Top-Secret Robot Notebook" right out of his hands.

"Hey, give me back my note-book!" said Eugene.

"No," said the cockroach, thumbing through the note-book. "This thing is great. A robot that eats your vegeta-bles, a robot that does your laundry, a robot that pushes everything under your bed."

"That's a Clean My Room Robot," Eugene interjected.

"Whatever. Here's a robot that has a pizza oven in its butt. I love this! It's mine!"

Cornelius scuttled down the hall with Eugene's notebook.

"When will I ever learn?" Eugene thought out loud. "Nice flies always finish last."

4

Eugene's First Friend

The next day, a new bug joined the class. His name was Fred Flea. He took the seat just behind Eugene's.

"Hey, I know you," said Eugene. "You're with the flea circus! My family loves the flea circus, and you're my sister's favorite!" Eugene didn't mention that Fred was also his favorite. It just didn't feel right.

"I'm glad you enjoyed the show," said Fred.

Eugene couldn't stop smiling, and he couldn't wait to tell Elle!

Mrs. Tiger Moth asked Fred to introduce himself to the class. He explained that he was late because he'd spent the morning helping his family pack up the flea circus. It would open again in the spring, but starting today Fred was a student like everyone else.

Everyone liked him right away. Everyone except Cornelius.

"You look like a runt if you ask me!" laughed the ginormous cockroach.

"I'm a flea," said Fred. "A normal-size flea."

"I bet you smell like a dog!" joked Cornelius.

"Probably," said Fred. "The circus travels by dog."

"Are you trying to be funny, Frank?" asked Cornelius.

"It's not Frank; it's Fred," said Fred. "And I'm not funny, but the clowns in our circus are hilarious. Why don't you see a show sometime? I'll get you a friend discount."

"I'm not your friend," replied Cornelius. "I would never be friends with a tick."

"I'm a flea," said Fred. "Ticks are much bigger and fatter."

"Hey! We're plump, not fat!" cried Todd Tick from the back of the room.

"Whatever! I wouldn't go to a flea circus if you paid me a million bucks!" shouted Cornelius. "Flea circuses are boring. Fleas are boring. And you, Floyd Flea, *are the most boring flea in the world!*"

"It's Fred," said Fred.

"Your name is whatever I decide to call you," said Cornelius. "And today your name is Frannie!"

And no one said a word, because even though they liked Fred, no one—not even Ted Tarantula, who was poisonous and bigger than Cornelius—had the courage to stand up to Cornelius.

In gym class that day, Coach Caterpillar split the class into two sides for dodge ball. Eugene was on Fred's team. Cornelius was on the other. It didn't take long for Cornelius to hit Eugene with the ball, knocking him out of the game. Again, Eugene wasn't the most athletic of bugs. But every time Cornelius threw the ball at Fred, he jumped out of the way. Soon the game was down to just two players: the giant roach and the normal-size flea.

The more Fred dodged, the angrier Cornelius got. After fifteen minutes of throwing the ball as hard as he could, Cornelius hunched over, exhausted, and Fred bounced the ball off the roach's head, ending the game. Eugene and Fred slapped high five with their teammates after their side won.

"I called time-out. I wasn't ready," Cornelius said.

"I didn't hear you call time-out," said Fred.

"That's because you have small ears!" screamed the roach. "If I say I called time-out, Fergus, I called time-out!"

"Well, maybe you should talk louder next time," said Fred. "And it's Fred, not Fergus."

"That's it! It is *on*," yelled Cornelius, as he headed straight toward Fred.

Just then, Coach Caterpillar blew his whistle and told the students to get ready to go back to class.

"You're mine, Ferris Flea!" howled Cornelius. "You and Billie Jean Epstein will know a world of hurt!"

"Billie Jean Epstein?" asked Fred.

"I think that's me," said Eugene.

They laughed.

They sat together at lunch and talked, and Eugene learned that Fred Flea wasn't one of those bugs that thought being smart makes you a nerd. Fred was one of those bugs that thought smart flies like Eugene were cool.

That was the day Eugene Flystein and Fred Flea became friends. Pest friends.

5

The Ultimo 6-9000

That afternoon, back at the Flystein house,
Eugene showed Fred some of
his inventions.
The Diapermatic
5000 was a
self-changing
diaper machine for
moms, while the
Booger Regenerator
789-A turned
boogers into

frozen pizzas that could be served to bugs in school cafeterias all over the world.

Fred was amazed with Eugene's creativity and his passion to change the world.

Then Eugene told Fred about his best invention yet: the Ultimo 6-9000. It was a machine that increased your abilities, like physical strength and intelligence, by 9,000 times! And it only took about six seconds to work (hence the name 6-9000), give or take a few seconds depending on things like temperature and body mass. The Ultimo 6-9000 would even the playing field against Cornelius if he threatened them again.

"Are you planning on going up against him?" asked Fred.

"Well, I don't think I have a choice. What if he would have hurt you today?" said Eugene.

Eugene showed Fred the Ultimo 6-9000, but to Fred, it didn't look like a high-tech gadget at all. And that's because it wasn't. In fact, it looked exactly like a piece of key lime pie. The Ultimo 6-9000 could be hidden in plain sight and no one would ever suspect a thing.

It looked so real and delicious that it took Fred all the willpower he had not to eat it. Fred wasn't sure if Eugene was a genius, a lunatic, or a future lunch lady.

The next day Eugene was suspicious when Cornelius wasn't on the school bus. Gossip traveled fast at Brown Barge, and the word in the hallways was that Cornelius was looking to settle the score with Eugene and Fred once and for all.

"He's out for blood," said Susie Spider.

"I'm always out for blood," said Monica Mosquito.

"I heard he's going to make them smell their own farts," said Frankie Firefly.

But Cornelius was nowhere to be found.

Later, Mrs. Tiger Moth was showing her students an educational film on the digestive systems of flies when she told the class she needed to step out for a moment to use the restroom. Eugene and Fred didn't think twice about it; tiger moths are known to have small bladders. But Eugene *was* surprised that within a few seconds, the door opened again.

He knew that something wasn't right. He could feel it in his exoskeleton. He smelled something awful, and this time it wasn't his mom's cooking.

Cornelius C. Roach stood in the doorway.

"Listen up, maggots!" yelled Cornelius as he flipped on the light switch. "The movie is over! Now who wants to see a live match of ultimate bug crunching?"

Before anyone could blink, the crazed cockroach had already picked up Eugene by his head and was squeezing it.

"Oh no!" said Eugene. "Quick, Fred, there's *pie* in my backpack!"

Fred knew instantly what Eugene *really* wanted. He grabbed Eugene's backpack off his desk and began frantically searching for the Ultimo 6-9000. If he could just throw it at Eugene—and if Eugene could taste even a little bit of it—then it would increase his strength 9,000 times!

In the meantime, Cornelius was using Eugene to erase the chalkboard.

"Fred!" cried Eugene. "A little help? There's only one piece of pie in my backpack!"

"I'm on it!" said Fred.

Fred found the Ultimo 6-9000 under some comic books in Eugene's backpack.

"Get ready to be exterminated, you stinking cockroach!" said Fred.

"Now," said Eugene. "My brain feels like mashed potatoes! Throw it at me now!"

Fred aimed and threw the Ultimo 6-9000 right at Eugene's head.

But Cornelius spun around at the last second, and the key lime pie hit him smack dab in his face. Oops.

The plan backfired!

Cornelius was about to get 9,000 times more powerful.

"What is going on in here?" shrieked Mrs. Tiger

Moth, returning from the restroom. "Why are you all out of your seats? Who made this mess?"

Eugene, thinking fast, grabbed Fred by the arm and approached their teacher. "It was us, Mrs. Tiger Moth," he said. "Fred and I are to blame for this mess, and to show you how sorry we are, we're going to the principal's office right now." He rushed out of the room, dragging Fred with him.

"Why did you say it was *our* fault?" asked Fred as the two bugs hurried down the hallway.

"Six seconds, remember?" said Eugene. "I thought we better get out of there before Cornelius goes from being a big bad cockroach to a *super* big bad cockroach."

"Good thinking," said Fred. "Lucky for us, I was able to pick this up off the floor when no one was looking."

Fred had retrieved the Ultimo 6-9000 without anyone noticing, and he now placed it in Eugene's hand. Eugene held up the slightly mushed piece of pie, inspecting it closely, and then smiled. He and Fred slapped high fives. Of course they still had to hope the principal took it easy on them.

Back in class, Mrs. Tiger Moth had restored order and was about to start a discussion on the film the class had been watching when Cornelius raised his hand.

"Yes, Cornelius?" said Mrs. Tiger Moth.

"I'd like to discuss the film," he said, even though he'd only seen about one second of it. But as he began to talk, it became very clear to his teacher and his classmates that he wasn't their normal thug bug. Cornelius C. Roach had suddenly become smart—9,000 times smarter, actually!

Lucy Kaboosie, the ladybug, saw Cornelius pull out the notebook he'd taken from Eugene and start to thumb through the pages.

"Cornelius?" asked Lucy. "You seem a little different. Are you feeling okay?"

"Never felt better," he said. "You know what's funny? I thought this notebook was full of cool drawings of robots, but now I realize that they're *design plans* for robots. I think I can build these."

And suddenly, even though she didn't understand why, Lucy felt very afraid.

6

Crazy Like a Cockroach

Principal Praying Mantis was a no-nonsense type, and he didn't earn his tough

reputation by taking it easy on bad bugs. He didn't tolerate shenanigans or funny business of any kind. School was for learning, not for horse-flying around. He sentenced both Eugene and Fred to detention.

While Eugene and Fred were in detention that afternoon, they talked about what would happen if the Ultimo 6-9000 had actually worked and turned Cornelius into a super bug.

"Can't we just reverse it?" asked Fred.

"It's not that easy," said Eugene.

That night their worst nightmare came true. Every television channel showed news reports of a massive crime spree happening all over Stinkopolis. The crimes were being committed by a new super villain the media was calling "Crazy Cockroach."

Reporter Alexander Aphid broadcasted: "This masked menace has been breaking into kitchens all over Stinkopolis, openly stealing while frightened bugs hide under their sinks. When local bug enforcement hit the burglar bug with a roach bomb, authorities say it didn't even faze the radical roach. He just laughed in their faces and escaped by flying through the ceiling."

Fred and Eugene watched in horror as live video footage showed a masked cockroach walking out of the smoke from a burning building and laughing at the Bug SWAT Team as he walked past them.

Eugene and Fred knew exactly who it was,

especially when the cockroach zipped off 9,000 times faster than its normal speed. The Bug Police, the Bug Army, the Bug SWAT Team, and the Bug Boy Scouts all tried to stop him, but they were no match. They hadn't seen anything like this before. And they definitely weren't prepared to deal with it.

7

The Fly Trap

The following morning, Eugene and Fred met at Fred's house before school and discussed their plan. They were going to track Cornelius down in a secret place and hit him with the Ultimo 6-9000 again. The night before they had worked late modifying the piece of pie, creating a reverse switch. Now the Ultimo 6-9000 would make Cornelius 9,000 times dumber, weaker, and slower in six seconds, turning him back into the normal giant bully cockroach he'd been before

all this craziness began. They just had to find Cornelius before he found them!

They got to school early, planning to sneak up on Cornelius, but they could never get him alone.

Finally, just when they were about to give up, Eugene saw Elle sitting by herself at a lunch table.

"Hey, there's Elle. Why is she sitting all alone? I'm going to talk to her," said Eugene. "Hold this!"

"What if while we were planning a trap for him, he was planning a trap for us?" Fred asked Eugene. "What if all of this is a fly trap?"

But Eugene wasn't listening. He was already halfway to Elle.

As soon as Eugene sat down next to Elle, Cornelius was there in a blink of an eye. Or in a fly's case, 800 eyes. Then even more bugs showed up. It was a bug bully bonanza!

All the bugs started pushing Eugene around as Elle pleaded for them to stop.

Then Fred heard Eugene say the strangest thing.

"I guess I'm going to have to teach you pesky pests a lesson once and for all!"

Fred wasn't sure how Eugene was going to teach anyone a lesson, especially since Fred was holding Eugene's backpack.

That's it! Fred thought. Eugene had realized it might be a trap and left his backpack with Fred on purpose. Eugene would create a diversion by putting himself into the hands of the bullies. That would give Fred the chance to use the Ultimo 6-9000 and change Cornelius back to normal. *Eugene's a genius!*

Fred pulled the Ultimo 6-9000 out and aimed carefully at Cornelius's head. This time he was going to make sure he hit his target.

Fred fired the pie right at the roach's face!

But the piece of key lime pie was no match for Cornelius. He saw it coming. The big roach moved aside in a flash, and the Ultimo 6-9000 hit the wall, bouncing off and hitting the floor.

Fred had one chance, and he'd blown it. Not only that—he smashed a perfectly good piece of pie.

Again!

8

Zero to Hero

Fred felt like all had been lost.

The next thing Fred saw was Eugene sailing past him.

BAM! Eugene smacked headfirst into the wall.

Fred looked on in horror.

"Graaab iiit!" Eugene yelled at Fred, pointing at the squashed Ultimo 6-9000 that was lying at Elle's feet. Cornelius was moving in for the kill.

With Cornelius bearing down on Eugene, Fred knew a pie in the roach's face could save the day. He had just about reached it when Elle picked it up.

"What's with this piece of pie, Fred? It's a little smushed, but it still looks delicious."

"It's not what you think, Elle. Please, give it to me now! Besides, uh, you wouldn't want to eat pie that's been crushed on the floor!"

"But I kind of do," said Elle as she reluctantly handed it to Fred. "I'm going to get help, Fred."

Elle took off to get help just as Eugene landed with a splash in a vat full of chocolate pudding. Just then, one of the hair-netted

lunch ladies scooped Eugene up and dumped him on a lunch tray.

Eugene was struggling to get the chocolate pudding off his legs and wings when Fred noticed Cornelius staring at Eugene as if he were lunch, licking his lips and rubbing his big bug belly. The look on Cornelius's face said, "Bon appétit!" He was about to eat chocolate pudding à la fly!

Cornelius coiled up like a rattlesnake preparing to strike.

"Mmm, I love chocolate pudding with a fly on top," mumbled the roach.

The Ultimo 6-9000 hit Eugene at the same time that Cornelius flew through the pudding with his mouth wide open. But instead of getting a mouthful of chocolate-pudding-covered fly, Cornelius only got a mouthful of pudding. The pie in the face had knocked Eugene out of the way just in time, as Cornelius smashed headfirst into the wall.

What no one saw (because it happened so fast) was that Fred had turned the Ultimo 6-9000 back to its original setting before throwing it, and in another six seconds Eugene was going to be 9,000 times better at flying, 9,000 times stronger, and 9,000 times faster! Fred had given his friend a fighting chance.

Suddenly a dark shadow fell over the flea.

"Cornelius is standing over me, ready to pounce, isn't he?" asked Fred as he gulped.

"Get ready to be squashed, Ferdinand!" said the angry cockroach.

"It's Fred!" said Fred.

Cornelius *pounced!*

But Fred was already gone.

Eugene had soared in like a super jet rocket, snatched up Fred, and flown straight through the roof! Before Fred opened his eyes to see if he was alive or inside Cornelius's belly, Eugene had flown him almost all the way to the moon.

When Elle returned with Coach Caterpillar and Principal Praying Mantis, the lunchroom was empty and the only sign there had been any trouble was the hole in the ceiling.

"That wasn't there when I left," Elle explained.

She had no idea what Eugene had become.

Because Eugene Flystein was no longer just a fly.

Eugene Flystein was a *super fly*!

9

Super Fly!

When Eugene and Fred finally made it back to the Flystein house after narrowly escaping the wrath of Cornelius, Eugene was so distracted that he ended up walking right through the door.

"Hey, you just walked through the front door," said Fred.

"Duh, how do you think we got in the house?" replied Eugene.

"No, you literally walked *through* the front door!" said Fred, pointing to the fly-shaped hole in the door.

"Oh no, what just happened?" asked Eugene.

"I just told you. You walked right through your door," explained Fred.

"My mom is going to kill me," said Eugene. "I've never been strong and fast before. I've never even considered myself remotely athletic."

Fred thought that was an understatement. He'd seen Eugene play dodge ball. It wasn't pretty.

Fred explained what it's like to be fast and

strong, since fleas are very fast and strong for their size.

"It must be pretty awesome to be you," said Eugene.

"It's pretty awesome," said Fred.

Eugene realized getting used to his new physical abilities would take some practice, and he wasn't sure how his family would feel about it, so he told Fred they would need to keep it a secret until Eugene could figure out how to tell them. Luckily, no one was home.

Fred suggested that Eugene zoom around the dump, find another door without a hole in it, and switch the doors.

Eugene did just that . . . all in eleven seconds.

"Pretty impressive," said Fred.

"I know, right?" said Eugene. "It's amazing how well I can see and how fast I can fly. I don't even think I need to wear these glasses anymore. But what will everyone say if I suddenly stop wearing my glasses?"

"Well for one they'd stop calling you Four Eyes," said Fred.

"They call me Four Eyes?" asked Eugene.

"Who cares?" said Fred. "The point is, you don't have to wear them when you're being a superhero," said Fred.

"A superhero? But I'm not a superhero," said Eugene. "I don't know anything about being a superhero."

"What's there to know? The big part is having superpowers, and that part is already done," said Fred. "Besides, who's going to stop Crazy Cockroach if you don't?"

"You're right, Fred. Crazy Cockroach is a problem we created," said Eugene.

"*We?*" asked Fred.

"Yes, we!" said Eugene. "You're the one that hit him with the Ultimo 6-9000."

"Because I was trying to save you!" said Fred.

"Yeah, thanks for that, by the way," said Eugene.

"You're welcome," said Fred.

That night Crazy Cockroach was at it again. The news reported that the villainous roach had stolen copper wire from construction

sites, raided a used appliance store, and cleaned out several hardware stores.

"He's up to something, but what?" said Eugene.

"You have to stop him," said Fred.

"Did you know the average life expectancy of a hippopotamus is forty to fifty years?"

"Don't change the subject," said Fred. "Sooner or later, the good superhero confronts the super villain."

"I've never heard that," Eugene said.

"Before that happens you'll need to come up with a disguise to hide who you really are," said Fred.

"I've heard of that," said Eugene. "Like they do in the movies and comic books!"

"And you'll need backup, a superhero sidekick," said Fred. "Someone brave enough to stare evil in the face without screaming for his mommy."

"Someone I can trust with my life," said Eugene.

"Exactly!" said Fred, clearly expecting Eugene to ask him to be his sidekick.

"And I'll need a superhero name," said Eugene. "Something cool and awesome that says, 'Don't mess with me or else!' A name that would make bullies like Crazy

Cockroach think long and hard before fighting me."

"Now that's what I'm talking about!" said Fred, still waiting for Eugene to ask him to tag along.

Eugene zipped off and returned a second later.

Only now he looked different. Eugene wore glasses, but now he did not. Eugene didn't wear a cape, but now he did. Well, it was actually a yellow tablecloth that Eugene borrowed from home, but it still looked like a cape—from a distance, at least.

But what really pulled the outfit all together was . . . the tights!

He had on tights Elle used to wear to dance class.

"How do I look?" said Eugene.

"You look like a professional dancer," said Fred, "or like a real-life superhero. What should I call you?"

"How about The Amazing, Awesome, Astonishing, Exciting, Extravagant, Fabulous, Wonderful, High-Flying, Death-Defying, Brilliant, Brainiac, Strongest Fly in the World . . . Fly?" said Eugene.

"How about Super Fly?" suggested Fred.

"Yeah, Super Fly works!" Eugene said.

"Now, how about that sidekick?" asked Fred.

"Actually, I gave it some more thought,"

said Eugene. "And I'm best when I work alone."

"But you need a *sidekick*," said Fred. "All superheroes have one!"

"You're right. Do you know anyone?" asked Eugene.

Disappointed, Fred got quiet and put his head down.

"I'm just teasing," Eugene said. "Of course it's you, silly! You're my best friend and the only one that knows who Super Fly really is.

"But you don't have to be my sidekick," Eugene went on. "We can be an equal team, fifty-fifty, two super-heroes fighting for truth, justice, and good bugs everywhere."

"Thanks," said Fred. "But you've got the

superpowers. Besides, I like being the side-kick. Less pressure if we mess up. Does this mean I have the job?"

"Of course," said Eugene.

"That's fantastic!" said Fred.

"And fantastic is what we'll call you," said Eugene. "You'll be known as Fantastic Flea."

"Sweet!" said Fred. "Now I have to work on my sidekick super suit. Does your sister have an extra pair of tights?"

"Let's look! Orange would look nice with your skin tone. Just saying," said Eugene.

10

Crazy Days and Crazy Nights

The world was in danger.

Crazy Cockroach was out of control and making life miserable for everyone. Bugs all over Stinkopolis complained about missing refrigerators and washing machines, stolen lawnmowers and televisions, and wires being ripped from the walls. They even complained about having tools stolen right out of their hands by the huge roach. Crazy Cockroach was getting worse day by day, but what was he planning?

At the end of the next school day, Eugene and Fred were spying on Cornelius and saw him drop some papers on the way to the bus. When Cornelius was far enough away they ran over, picked up the papers, and read them.

Crazy Cockroach's evil plan to rule the world:

1. Steal stuff to make army of robots.
2. Kidnap Elle so a dumb fly will try to rescue her at the main Stinkopolis garbage dump.
3. Go to school and drop plans to take over world so Stupid Fly and Fanspasmic Flea find them and will know where to find me and try to stop me.
4. Eat lunch. Maybe a salad? I need some fiber, feeling a little bloated lately.
5. Destroy the fly and the flea.
6. Unleash my robots on the world.
7. Rule the world.

"You know what this means, right?" said Eugene.

"That Crazy Cockroach is constipated?" said Fred.

"No. I mean, maybe, but it also means Crazy Cockroach has Elle!" said Eugene.

"Sweet chipmunk coffee-covered corn cobs, Super Fly!" said Fantastic Flea.

"Why are you talking like that?" asked Super Fly.

"Like what?" asked Fantastic Flea.

"Whatever. Let's find Elle!" said Super Fly.

"Great hairy hamster hiccups!" said the flea.

"Okay, you're doing it again," said Super Fly.

"It's the way sidekicks talk," said Fantastic Flea. "Everyone knows that."

"I see," said Super Fly. "Well, let's find Elle."

"Curdled corn chips, smelly armpits!" said Fantastic Flea.

"Seriously?" asked Super Fly.

"I'll stop," said Fantastic Flea.

Finally, they found Elle right where Crazy Cockroach's plans said she'd be. She was tied to a mousetrap and sleeping like a baby. And it looked like she had been sprinkled with Parmesan cheese.

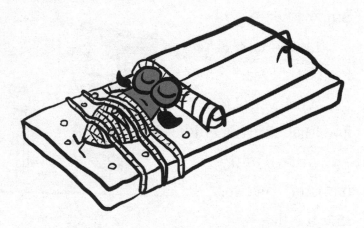

"Oh no!" cried Super Fly. "Crazy Cockroach has tied Elle to a mousetrap, and she's the cheese!"

This would have been a good time for

Fantastic Flea to say one of his silly sidekick lines, but he was too horrified to speak.

Crazy Cockroach had created giant robot rats that loved the taste of cheese, and the robots were headed straight for Elle.

"Eat the brat!" Crazy Cockroach commanded the robot rats.

Super Fly scooped up Fantastic Flea in his cape and used it as a sling to shoot him right at Crazy Cockroach.

"**BAMMO!**" shouted Fantastic Flea, bouncing off Crazy Cockroach's head.

"You're just a flea," said Crazy Cockroach. "I barely felt that!"

"Whatever. You might

want to take a look at your giant robot rats!" said Fantastic Flea.

Crazy Cockroach looked over to see that Elle was no longer in the mousetrap and his beloved robot rats were now reduced to pieces of twisted metal scattered across the ground.

"Rats!" yelled Crazy Cockroach.

There was no sign of Elle or Super Fly anywhere.

"Argh!" cried the cockroach. "Where are you, Super Fly? Are you too chicken to fight me?"

SLAM!

A broken-down old rust bucket of a school bus landed right on top of Crazy Cockroach.

Fantastic Flea looked up to see Super Fly hovering overhead, holding the still-sleeping Elle with one arm.

"Did you just pick up a school bus with one arm and drop it on Crazy Cockroach while you were rescuing Elle at the same time?" asked Fantastic Flea.

"I did," said Super Fly.

"What's going on? Who are you?" said Elle, waking up and starting to cry. "This is the worst nightmare ever. Hey, I have those same tights! Can you take me home, Mr. . . . Mr. . . . uh—"

"Just call me Super Fly," he said. "I'll be back, Fantastic Flea. Let me take her home. Keep an eye out for the roach."

Super Fly blasted off with a sonic boom.

Fantastic Flea, figuring the roach was smashed flat, decided to take a nap on a bubble gum wrapper. After all, superhero work can be exhausting.

That's when he heard what sounded like a helicopter; only it wasn't a helicopter at all. Fantastic Flea looked up to see a giant horsefly robot hovering above him. He thought he might still be dreaming when it shot lasers out of its eyes and breathed fire from its mouth, narrowly missing him!

"Mommy!" shouted Fantastic Flea, dodging fire and laser beams by leaping as fast and as high as he could, looking down to see

Crazy Cockroach crawling out from under the bus with a remote control in his hand.

"Man, cockroaches are hard to kill," said Fantastic Flea. And, fearing for his life, he did the only thing he could think of, heading out of the dump with the giant horsefly hot on his trail, hoping to draw the danger away from the good bugs of the city.

As fast and as far as Fantastic Flea jumped, the horsefly robot continued to close in on him.

"Gosh, horsefly robots are fast!" said Fantastic Flea, just as it caught up to him.

It looked like Fantastic Flea was done for. "Good-bye, cruel world," said Fred, fearing his time was up.

"I'm back!" shouted Super Fly.

And at the last possible moment Super Fly knocked Fantastic Flea free!

As Super Fly spun wildly in the air, he saw Fantastic Flea bounding through the open window of a human's house. His flea friend had left the safety of the dump and had entered the world of giants.

Fantastic Flea had accidentally jumped right into an enormous ceiling fan and hit the floor dazed and confused. Then something lifted him up.

"Super Fly? Is that you?"

No such luck. It was the giant horsefly, getting ready to bite him in half.

Once again, Super Fly managed to rescue his friend, snatching him from the giant horsefly's mouth, just as it chomped down with a *crunch!*

Super Fly jetted back outside toward safety, but just as they got to the edge of Stinkopolis, something grabbed him in midflight and started taking him down. Super Fly did his best to protect Fantastic Flea, dropping him onto a pile of old mattresses.

This time the menacing metallic robot had Super Fly, and he knew he was on his own. Using his best fake and spin move, Super Fly broke free with a supersonic burst of speed. A second later the horsefly robot was right behind him. That thing had turbo thrusters!

Super Fly headed back to the edge of the dump, back to the giant's house. It was his only hope.

Super Fly remembered seeing a box fan whirling in the house. He'd felt the cooling air coming from the machine's huge rotating blades. It made sense. It was a hot summer. It was a pretty impressive invention, even to a super-genius inventor.

Super Fly had to get to the fan before the robot got to him. He could fly through it, and the giant horsefly robot would follow him. It was a risky move, but he didn't have too many options. The blades could slice Super Fly into smithereens. His timing had to be perfect.

Super Fly flew headfirst through the box fan. The whirling blades just missed cutting Super Fly in half, but the bigger mechanical bug behind him was not so lucky. The sharp metal fan blades struck the horsefly robot with such force that it was destroyed completely on impact.

Super Fly bent down and looked into one of the robot's eyes as the light flickered on and off for the last time. "Hey, Crazy Cockroach! How do you like me now?"

"**NO! NO! NO!**" screamed Crazy Cockroach, who'd been watching every move from his secret lair. "I want that fly dead. I want Super Fly crushed! Darn you, Super Fly!"

11

Your Fly Is Down

Slightly injured where the blades of the fan had struck him, Super Fly limped back to the dump and toward home. He had to find Fantastic Flea and stop Crazy Cockroach.

Then he smelled it. It was a hint of an odor that turned into a full-on fragrance.

It was putrid rotting garbage.

"I could use a little fuel," Super Fly said to himself. "Being a superhero takes a lot out of you."

Super Fly couldn't know he was falling for

a trap. Crazy Cockroach had put a new invention to work, a mechanized Superduper Fly Swatter. He had positioned it on a mountain of garbage that sat in the middle of the dump.

Crazy's plan was simple: pile up a fly's favorite rotting food and put it right beneath his Superduper Fly Swatter. Super Fly would be lured in by the foul smell and be doomed.

Now, even though Super Fly was a genius times 9,000, he still couldn't fight his natural instincts. One good whiff was all it took to bring him to the largest steaming pile of garbage he'd ever seen in his whole life. It felt like his birthday. He didn't suspect a thing.

As he began to feast, the Superduper Fly Swatter came roaring down like a hurricane wind, fast and furious and full of anger. He never knew what hit him.

Swat!

When Super Fly awoke he smelled the most awful, horrible, vile, disgusting odor known to a fly's nose. Especially to a Super Fly that can smell 9,000 times better than the average fly.

Flowers.

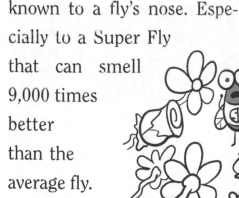

Flowers might smell pretty to us humans, but to a fly, it's the worst possible smell.

Crazy Cockroach had planned it perfectly. He'd planted a circle of giant, colorful flowers, a prison made specifically for Super Fly.

Sweet-smelling flowers were like kryptonite to Super Fly. Super Fly was no match for this kind of power. He felt too weak to move.

Crazy Cockroach walked over to Super Fly with a clothespin over his nose. Roaches aren't too fond of flowers either.

"*Nanny, nanny, boo, boo, someone got tricked, and we both know who, who!*" sang Crazy Cockroach. He added, "The final stage of my plan is about to begin."

Super Fly struggled to get up, but it wasn't happening.

"Super Fly has paid the price," sang Crazy Cockroach, *"for always being good and nice! Super Fly can't stop me now. And if he could, would he know how? Before this cockroach rules the Earth, I'm going to destroy it first!"*

Super Fly had no idea that Crazy Cockroach could sing like that. Not too shabby for an evil villain. He'd definitely be fun to do karaoke with sometime.

And then our hero fly was out like a light.

Crazy Cockroach knew his plan of turning the world into a cockroach paradise was within his grasp. There was one little thing he had to get rid of . . .

HUMANS! Dun, dun, *dun*.

12

A World of Hurt

Okay, so where were we? Oh, right.

Super Fly is trapped and defeated. Fantastic Flea is nowhere to be found. Crazy Cockroach has won, our superheroes have lost, evil is about to run wild, and the world as we know it will end. Good-bye, world. Hello, cockroach-infested planet of misery, and decay. No more birthday parties or birthday cake. No more chocolate chip ice cream. No more pizza. No more kickball. No more TV, movies, or video games. No more anything fun. All is lost.

Crazy Cockroach held the special doomsday remote control he had created for this exact moment. With a push of a button, he could unleash eight indestructible cockroach robots that looked just like him. What an ego! They were all programmed to do one thing: **DESTROY THE WORLD.**

Crazy Cockroach felt unstoppable and unbeatable. "I'm unstoppable and unbeatable!" he shouted.

And then he pushed the flashing red button.

Within minutes, the eight cockroach robots were smashing buildings and crushing

cars all around the world. Crazy Cockroach's crazy plan to rule the world was in full effect.

What Crazy Cockroach didn't know was that Fantastic Flea was alive and well. You remember Super Fly had dropped him on old mattresses, right? Sure, Fantastic Flea had a minor scuffle with some bedbugs for invading their turf, but once he explained what was happening, well, even bedbugs hate crazy cockroaches trying to take over the world. The bedbugs said they wanted to help, so Fantastic Flea made a plan on used toilet paper.

Fantastic Flea's Plan:

1. FIND SUPER FLY.
2. FREE SUPER FLY.
3. SUPER FLY SAVES THE WORLD.

Fantastic Flea and the bedbugs rushed to find Super Fly. When they finally found him, it was worse than they could have imagined.

"Oh no—flowers!" said Fantastic Flea. "The sweet smell is too much for his super senses. He needs stink! Grab anything that reeks of stench and follow me!"

The bedbugs were smart and quickly enlisted help.

In almost no time, an army of stinkbugs, lice, army ants, termites, ticks, and chiggers joined the mission to free Super Fly. They brought stinky pieces of moldy food, rotting

meats, fungus, and loads of dog poop—a favorite of all flies.

On Fantastic Flea's orders they covered the flowers in all of the stink and stench they could unload. The supreme stink made its way to the nose of the fallen fly. First he sniffed, then he coughed, then he gagged, and then Super Fly woke up! Super Fly was back!

Fantastic Flea hugged his best friend and helped him to his feet.

"Ding-dong donkey donuts, Super Fly!" cried Fantastic Flea. "Crazy Cockroach has unleashed an army of eight indestructible cockroach robots on the world!"

"I see you're back to using those slogans again, huh?" said Super Fly.

"Oh, I forgot. My bad," said Fantastic Flea.

"No, it's cool," said Super Fly. "Wait, did you say eight indestructible cockroach robots?"

"That's right, and they're zooming all over the world wreaking havoc, tearing down buildings, crushing bridges and tunnels. We have to destroy them!"

"But we can't," said Super Fly. "They're indestructible."

"Indestructible," said Fantastic Flea, realizing what the word really means.

"I should know," said Super Fly. "I designed them."

"What can *we* do?" asked the army of bugs that had come to Super Fly's aid.

"Nothing," said Super Fly.

"Nothing?" asked Fantastic Flea, but he knew that what Super Fly really meant was that no matter what they did, they couldn't stop indestructible robots. There was nothing to be done.

"Wait," said Super Fly. "I can't destroy

indestructible robots, but I can destroy the cockroach controlling them!" And he soared off into the sky.

"Where's he going?" asked everyone.

"He's going to save the world!" said Fantastic Flea.

13

Super Fly Saves the World

New York, Los Angeles, Chicago, London, Paris, Rome, Moscow, and Beijing were burning. The cockroach robots had moved on to Hong Kong, Taipei, Tokyo, Singapore, Sydney, Buenos Aires, Rio de Janeiro, and Clearwater, Florida—they have nice beaches there.

There was no stopping them. The police had tried, the firemen had tried, and even the meter maids had jumped in to help.

The Air Force had attacked, the Navy had attacked, the Army had attacked, and the Coast Guard had attacked. The Marines were *still* attacking! Nothing came close to stopping the robots.

Super Fly moved through the sky like a bullet. He had remembered the tracking device he'd stuck on Crazy Cockroach's back at the fly trap.

It gave Super Fly the exact location of the evil cockroach's lair.

The look on Crazy Cockroach's face when Super Fly burst through the ceiling of his lair was priceless.

"How did you escape my fly trap? How did you find me? Why did you put a huge hole in my ceiling? You've ruined my lair!" shouted Crazy Cockroach. "Seriously, I just had this place painted."

"I had help from the one thing you don't have—friends! Well, and also a tracking device," said Super Fly. "You need more than a bunch of flowers to get rid of me, Cornelius."

"Don't call me Cornelius, Super Fly. I mean, *Eugene*," replied Crazy, making a dash for the door.

Before the roach could escape, Super Fly grabbed Crazy Cockroach and headed straight into the sky.

"Put me down!" demanded Crazy Cockroach. "I have a world to conquer!"

Super Fly knew the robots were indestructible, but the remote that controlled them wasn't. He just had to get that remote.

"Hand me the remote and I will!" said Super Fly.

"Never!" said the roach, clutching the

remote and laughing maniacally. "You can't stop my robots!"

"Well, technically they're my robots, seeing as I designed them," said Super Fly.

Super Fly tried everything he could think of to get Crazy Cockroach to drop the remote. He tried tickling him, telling knock-knock jokes, and blowing in his ear. Nothing was working.

Super Fly was getting desperate. Who knew cockroaches weren't ticklish? Just then he thought of one more idea.

And it was at that precise moment, at the edge of where the Earth's atmosphere meets space, that Super Fly turned Crazy Cockroach loose. He simply let go, dropped him, and let him fall. And as soon as Crazy Cockroach started to plummet to the Earth, he let go of the remote.

"Heeelllppp!" screamed Crazy Cockroach.

Super Fly caught the remote in midair and quickly used it to shut down the robots.

All over the world, the cockroach robots turned off one by one.

Meanwhile, Crazy Cockroach was plummeting to Earth like a meteor, heading straight for Stinkopolis.

"Look," said Fantastic Flea. "Crazy Cockroach has been defeated! Super Fly has saved the world!"

Every bug in Stinkopolis cheered. "Super Fly! Super Fly! Super Fly!"

Super Fly wasn't finished yet. He caught Crazy Cockroach just before the big roach crashed into an old refrigerator in the middle of the dump. Like a rocket, Super Fly zoomed straight back up into the sky, with Crazy Cockroach in tow.

This time he did not stop at the edge of the Earth's atmosphere where the sky meets space. This time Super Fly flew beyond our planet and set his sights on the moon.

"Where are you taking me?" cried Crazy Cockroach.

"To a place where you can't hurt anybody ever again," said Super Fly.

"Uranus?" said Crazy Cockroach.

"No, somewhere not so gassy!" said Super Fly.

Super Fly took him to the one place where he couldn't hurt anyone, not even a flea:

The moon.

"Don't leave me here, Super Fly! Or when I get back to Stinkopolis, I'll, I'll . . ."

And right then a giant moon rock crashed down on the exact spot where Crazy Cockroach was standing.

14

Born to Fly

It didn't take long for word to spread all over Stinkopolis that Super Fly and Fantastic Flea had saved the world.

Mayor Kaboosie (Lucy the ladybug's dad) was so grateful that he decided to honor the heroes with a parade. He also made plans to award Super Fly and Fantastic Flea with the keys to the city, the highest honor the mayor could give the brave bugs that had risked their lives to protect the good bugs of Stinkopolis and the people of the world. It didn't matter if you were a cricket or a crane fly, a mosquito or a moth, a termite or a tiger beetle—every bug that could walk, crawl, or fly was going to be there.

School was even canceled so all the children of Stinkopolis could attend the parade. And what a parade it was! The leaf-cutting ants and metalwork butterflies had built parade floats, and animal balloons trailed along behind them. The marching band from the high school played "We Are the Champ Bugs" by Queen Bee, and mounted mealworms rode along on horseflies while planthopper police bugs shrilled like sirens and lightning bugs lit the way.

Eugene and Fred were in a bit of a predicament, though. Mr. and Mrs. Flystein had given them the job of keeping an eye on Elle.

"Oh, great," whispered Fred so only Eugene could hear him. "How are Super Fly and Fantastic Flea going to make an appearance if the two of us are babysitting?"

"You're right," said Eugene under his breath. "There's no way Super Fly and

Fantastic Flea can be honored by the mayor if they never show up."

"So *do something*," said Fred. "Eugene? Eugene?"

"Hey, Fred, where did Eugene go?" asked Elle.

Fred had turned away for a split second, and now Eugene was gone. Before Fred could figure out what had just happened, a loud roar came up from the crowd. Everyone was looking up to the sky.

Super Fly was flying loop de loops to the excited cheers of the adoring bugs below.

"Oh, come on!" said Fred. "Are you kidding me?"

"Oh, look!" cried Elle. "Eugene's missing Super Fly!"

Super Fly did a couple of cool aerial tricks and then landed on the grandstand to the delight of the crowd. Lucy Kaboosie swooned at the sight of him.

The mayor spoke into the microphone. "Welcome home, Super Fly. As mayor of Stinkopolis, and your biggest fan, I'd like to present you with the key to the city." Super Fly accepted it. The crowd went wild.

"Where is your other half?" asked the mayor. "Where's that fantastic sidekick of yours?"

"Fantastic Flea is probably chewing on a dog somewhere," said Super Fly. "I'll go get him." And Super Fly zoomed away.

"Wow, look at him go," said Elle.

"He's amazing, right?" asked Eugene.

Elle was surprised to see Eugene standing next to her in the same spot Fred had been a few seconds ago.

Just then the crowd cheered as Fantastic Flea bounded out of nowhere and landed on stage next to Mayor Kaboosie and Lucy.

"Sorry I'm late," said Fantastic Flea. "When ya gotta go, ya gotta go!"

The crowd burst into laughter, and even the mayor chuckled.

Fantastic Flea accepted his own key to the city and shook the mayor's hand. The crowd went wild.

"Oh no! Fred's missing Fantastic Flea," said Elle, looking over just as Fred came walking up.

It didn't take Elle long to notice that now Eugene was gone and Super Fly was flying over the cheering crowd again. She also noticed that Fantastic Flea had disappeared.

Could Eugene and Fred actually be Super Fly and Fantastic Flea? she wondered.

"Fred?" she asked. "Can I ask you a question?"

"Sure," said Fred.

"Will you hold my hand?"

"Sure," said Fred, taking Elle's hand.

Loud cheers rose from the crowd as Super Fly landed on the stage again next to Mayor Kaboosie and his daughter. Lucy leaned over and gave Super Fly a kiss on the cheek. The crowd went wild.

Not a bad day to be a superhero.

15

Back to School

A strange thing happened around school once Cornelius wasn't around to bully everyone anymore. It was peaceful. Bugs were kind. The wasps stopped stinging and the bed-bugs stopped biting, the mosquitoes weren't

sucking blood and the army ants weren't fighting. Even the hornets and the wasps were getting along.

Only Eugene and Fred knew that Cornelius wasn't coming back as long as Crazy Cockroach was stranded on the moon. But what Eugene and Fred didn't realize was that roaches aren't that easy to get rid of.

Cockroaches have been around since the dinosaur days for a reason. If Eugene and Fred had taken the time to look at the moon through Eugene's telescope, they might have noticed the movement of a moon rock. They might have seen a roach leg stretching out from beneath and scratching its way out, first with two legs digging, then three, then six . . .

A week before Halloween, the bugs of Brown Barge were getting excited about the night of candy to come. In Mrs. Tiger Moth's class, the teacher was calling the morning roll.

"Precious Butterfly."

"Here," said Precious.

"Bubba Beetle."

"Here," said Bubba.

"Carlos Caterpillar."

"Present," said Carlos.

"Reed Centipede."

"Yo," said Reed.

"Cornelius C. Roach."

"Cornelius C. Roach."

"Cornelius . . ."

Mrs. Tiger Moth looked up from the roll and right at Eugene and Fred for a moment. Did she know something? Eugene looked over his shoulder at Fred. Fred shrugged. Eugene rolled his eyes.

Finally, Mrs. Tiger Moth looked toward the empty desk in the back of the room and called his name one last time.

"Cornelius C. Roach."

"Here."

Mrs. Tiger Moth looked up.

Every bug in the class looked up.

"No way," said Eugene.

"Oh no," said Fred.

Every bug in the room cringed at the sight of the all-too-familiar figure walking through the doorway.

Cornelius C. Roach was back.

Todd H. Doodler is the author and illustrator of *Rawr!* and the Bear in Underwear series, as well as many other fun books for young readers. He is also the founder of David & Goliath, a humorous T-shirt company, and Tighty Whitey Toys, which makes plush animals in underwear. He too is a part-time superhero and lives in Los Angeles with his daughter, Elle, and their two labradoodles, Muppet and Pickleberry.